Para todos los gatos gordos...

for fat cats everywhere...

xist Publishing

Mi gato es gordo
My Cat is Fat

By Katrina Streza
illustrated by Brenda Ponnay

Mi gato es gordo.

My cat is fat.

Yo tengo un gato gordo.

I have a fat cat.

¿Ves a mi gato?

Do you see my cat?

¡No! Ese no es mi gato.

No! That is not my cat.

Ese es un perro triste. Mi gato no es un perro triste.

That is a sad dog.
My cat is not a sad dog.

¿Ves a mi gato?

Do you see my cat?

¡No! Ese no es mi gato.

No! That is not my cat.

Ese es un cerdo grande.
Mi gato no es un cerdo
grande.

That is a big pig.
My cat is not a big pig.

¿Ves a mi gato?

Do you see my cat?

¡No! Ese no es mi gato.

No! That is not my cat.

Ese es un zorrillo apestoso.
Mi gato no es un zorrillo
apestoso.

That is a stinky skunk.
My cat is not a stinky skunk.

¿Ves a mi gato?

Do you see my cat?

¡No! Ese no es mi gato.

No! That is not my cat.

Ese es un pez plano.
Mi gato no es un pez plano.

That is a flat fish!
My cat is not a flat fish.

¿Ves a mi gato?

Do you see my cat?

¡No! Ese no es mi gato.

No! That is not my cat.

Ese es un pequeño pato.
Mi gato no es un pequeño pato.

That is a little duck.
My cat is not a little duck.

¿Ves a mi gato?

Do you see my cat?

¡No! Ese no es mi gato.

No! That is not my cat.

Esa es una rana roja.
Mi gato no es una rana roja.

That is a red frog.
My cat is not a red frog.

¡Ese es mi gato!

That is my cat!

Yo tengo un gato gordo.

I have a fat cat.

CPSIA information can be obtained
at www.ICGtesting.com
Printed in the USA
LVOW05s2300230118
563790LV00020B/63/P